Muse, maestra, myself to you, that I might find
(please) both fire and thorn with simplest ease.

CONTENTS

ALL THE USELESS THINGS ARE MINE

A BOOK OF SEVENTEENS

THOMAS WALTON

ETCHINGS & DRAWINGS BY
DOUGLAS MILLER

Sagging Shorts

Set in Van Dijck MT with LaTeX.

ISBN: 978-1-944697-91-4 (paperback)
ISBN: 978-1-944697-89-1 (ebook)
Library of Congress Control Number: 2020933070

Sagging Meniscus Press
Montclair, New Jersey
saggingmeniscus.com

ALL
THE
USELESS
THINGS
ARE
MINE

AT THE CRACK OF UP

So the sky turned light this morning, night ended. *You* didn't have anything to do with it.

In the dream the whales were breaching and someone shouted, "what the fluke!" I was the sea.

It dawned on me when the sun finally lifted clear of the neighbors' platoon of shivering poplars.

I didn't mean to vomit on the dentist, but I couldn't quite swallow his blue rubber hands.

My dictionary says Ovid's known for his "explorations of love" whereas I'm known for flatulations of it.

I will find a new way, one they say I can't go, one I imagine for myself.

Little man in enormous truck shouts: I don't have a Napoleon complex! . . . it's much bigger than that.

I asked her what the book was like, and she said "oh kind of like mid-century modern."

I sat all night watching the soft rain showering the streetlights glowing as night dreamt of morning.

Again

The smell of flowers woke me up, and I realized I'd passed out in the neighbor's rosebushes.

. . .

The blue light was so blue this morning when the blue light grew in place of black.

. . .

I wonder if people talk about me secretly, or if they do so without secreting at all.

. . .

Someone should take notes when the sun comes up, so we never forget how gorgeous it is.

. . .

Fortunately I was able to unscrew it before the police showed up with Rabbi Steiner's cow bell.

. . .

It's not the sky that's blue every morning but every single shiver of every speck of air.

. . .

In the restaurant the baby was so terribly ugly my mashed potatoes seemed, even, to radiate beauty.

. . .

The sun came up and with it all the sleeping people concerned with everything but the sun.

We buried the rainclouds under the dogwood with a sign that read: Here Lies Last Night's Storm.

. . .

I just woke up when I noticed out the kitchen window: a huge tower of glimmering flapjacks.

. . .

This morning it struck me that we're all like awful aubades: torn from our beds at dawn.

. . .

Sure it's fun to play pretend, to wear a balloon hat and ride a porcupine to school.

. . .

Do you really think this is the only chance you have at life, just one, then . . . nothing?

. . .

I wonder if you can still buy beachballs—do they exist?—now that I'm living in Wyoming.

. . .

Nobody tells you the morning light is blue, bluer than the bluest blue moon. Nobody says that.

. . .

Jordan was just sitting there knitting when a large blue stallion galloped in, dead as the moon.

. . .

At the river mouth the river calmly lamented, "strange how everything seems to have gone down hill."

Dear Pencil, forgive me for ruining your happy lovely graphite singing with my plastic mumble. Sincerely, Keyboard.

. . .

When the sun rose the fire hydrants all opened their arms and smiled dancing wild green pirouettes.

. . .

What I need is just one more morning, scribbling there, the radio towers flashing through the fog.

. . .

Every morning the neighbors leave their flats and cadaver off to work so mechanical and thoughtless bored.

. . .

When the sun broke like an egg over the field I just ate and ate and ate.

. . .

I ran out of the garden screaming, "the hydrangea's blooming! the hydrangea's blooming!" pants around my knees.

. . .

After listening to all she was said to have said, the girl at the picnic said nothing.

. . .

At five a.m. it's dark, by seven all the books glimmer in the newly lambent morning light.

When the sunlight spills over the brick building the purple flowers purple there grow purple even more.

. . .

The stairs behind the museum in the park evidently are a great place to take a shit.

. . .

Windows rattle in a heavy gale, excited the sun has come (again) to give us another chance.

. . .

I went to the Wildlife Refuge unsure whether I should merely visit or commit myself at length.

. . .

It was striking how the eggs kept frying after the storm blew the oak onto the house.

. . .

After the rain, everything on our street sighed, we all breathed in, we all woke up again.

July 5

The morning after, fireworks lay dead on the ground near the hydrangea's sparkling clusters of spinning flowers.

. . .

The first chill autumn nights now cold as a zombie stumbling in to breathe on the geraniums.

. . .

I watched a vulture circling slowly around the neighbor lady pacing on her newly painted widow's walk.

. . .

We sat in the shade and watched the Staten Island Ferry crossing just ahead of the storm.

. . .

The green water holds well a white sailboat proud as a clit in the thickly wooded cove.

. . .

Beside the easy flow of the shallow creek the easy flow of the round rocks waved hello.

. . .

The frost seized last night the scarlet petals of the geranium spilling through the iron balcony rail.

. . .

The weatherman said the clouds'll soon dissipate and the sky will open like a great glowing clam.

I love the way the sea and surf are such a necessary nightmare devouring us in waves.

The one bare tree yesterday is now suddenly a thousand flowers fluttering in a single February breeze.

All day we drove and all day the sagebrush clumps on the far hills drove with us.

The great thing about a marsh is that it's always singing, even when it's still it's singing.

When the wind stripped the dogwood of leaves it covered itself with starlings and timidly staggered away.

Ahead of the storm the elm tree shattered into a hundred thousand fluttering seeds flattering the air.

All morning rain grey as a seal sigh misted the garden until sunlight finally burst laughing through.

The mountain said with perfect clarity (though without words) "a moment is merely a movement of light."

The storm passed and when it did it left the plum tree bedazzled as a spinning child.

I like to think the willow's tresses breathe in the wind, and then breathe the wind away.

. . .

The kids were playing by the river when the little one fell in, drifted out, then disappeared.

. . .

It's only March but I'm already dreaming of dahlias splashing the hillside near where the drunkards piss.

. . .

The flooded ditch was so clear you could see the carrot flowers waving desperately as they drowned.

. . .

Quiet morning, placid bay, reflecting cedar trees, when the whale breaks the surface it shatters the sea.

. . .

Coming at last out of the dense forest, a meadow, and in it a single rusting Mitsubishi.

. . .

All the maple seeds in the sugar maple cluttered the air when the dump truck rattled by.

. . .

Barn Burner
The bare branches of the maple flare up against the grey paint peeling off the rotting barn.

Along the neighbor's stairs, the morning light has married the clematis vine twining its black iron rail.

. . .

Don't be afraid of doing nothing, walking quiet on a morning trail, winter wren, Solomon's seal, salal.

. . .

We rode all day, our bikes beneath us, redbuds blooming along the eerily empty affluent neighborhood streets.

. . .

In the bay the tugboat tugged, rope taut, pulling Jordan's swollen member beneath a gull-plagued, Titian sky.

. . .

We set our blanket and our picnic basket down, thermos of iced coffee, on the subway seat.

. . .

Carpe Diem
The blue sea this morning laps around a guano-stained rock that catches all the sun it can.

. . .

They found the clothes behind the fence and the body in the iberis being eaten by hornets.

. . .

Over the city a plane flew in a wide elegant circle, sunlight flashing off its silver wing.

I love the way that autumn flares up in a ubiquity of dying, every flower falling over.

The rain never let the sun rise so all the grey enokidake huddled under Jordan's new car.

When the sun rose over the hill, the frost-covered rooftops started steaming in the ice-clear glittering air.

HALITOSES

I saw the school bus passing by, so yellow, so sad when it disappeared into the lake.

The river slowed at its bend, widening as it chewed dirt from the buried girl scout's head.

The one who so desperately tries to blend in may as well be desolated in a blender.

The word "pandemonium" comes from Milton, his Capitol of Hell: privet hedge when the flowers open up.

They found the little boy's arm in the ceanothus, busy with light blue flowers and happy bees.

It was delightful how the neighbors' garage collapsed like a flim cardhouse when the oak branch fell.

The sky was all Wellesley girls and badminton in the terrible dream where you were Hillary Clinton.

Just So You Know
In the insufferable tedium of the post office line it wasn't me who pooped in his pants.

Jordan has trouble staying on the wagon when it's raining or she might be breathing sometime soon.

. . .

I love the way the rancid smell of linden trees questions the assumption of sweet smelling flowers.

. . .

Does the "five second rule" apply when someone drops their phone, can you quickly eat it then?

I walked up to school to meet her, to walk her home in the wild swirling snow.

The thorny hedge makes a mess of little kids when you throw them in it after dinner.

If We Owned a House
She said "oh yes and we could get a tiny pony" as if that would be heaven.

My daughter said the dead body is under the desk rotting in the shape of a pear.

I hope I'm wrong about you getting older and full of holes like the rest of us.

A wind rose, a gale, and when it finally subsided (it never did) you were grown, gone.

For twelve years we laughed, cried, sang, played, painted, puzzled, and climbed, but then she just forgot.

On the promontory far in the distance, the tiny woman throws the tiny baby into the sea.

I was about to tell her why she couldn't when a little breeze blew in, saying "sshhhhh."

. . .

I watched you play for eleven years at the dollhouse that now you say is "for babies."

. . .

I picked out a pony for your birthday, but it died when the barn caught on fire.

. . .

Some seals were splashing around out near the piles where that woman tied her kids last year.

. . .

Night Night (Lord of the Flies)
I just finished reading my daughter the chapter where the severed pig's head tells Simon to run.

. . .

Our babysitter drinks whiskey and is usually late, but we don't mind, we don't have a baby.

. . .

I try to explain that math equations are exercises in achieving harmony when she screams, "fuck you!"

. . .

We spent all day on the lawn making daisy-chains, each one a miracle we'd never see again.

We watched some fire ants carry a moth down into the sidewalk crack, then both started crying.

. . .

Now suppose there are pigeons you spend all afternoon plucking and pulling from your dead daughter's hair.

. . .

Think of This in Math Class If You Get Bored
All the blond dry grasses shoot up like pikes, each one dripping with pretty little decapitated heads.

. . .

I couldn't sleep so I shoved all my horrors beneath the bed and walked her to school.

. . .

Remember? You were barely any taller than the daisies we would gather from the fields and riverbanks?

. . .

When the darkness comes, remember these little dreams, these little light rings we've made in the pool.

. . .

Off You Go
Don't forget your lunch, your backpack and clarinet, and to live knowing that you'll soon be dead.

I remember one Christmas when my brother ate cat shit because I told him it was gravy.

· · ·

Our faces grimaced when my grandfather slit its throat and the hog drained, my sisters' and mine.

· · ·

You're so Handsome
I saw your comment about me on Facebook, you better knock that shit off right now . . . mom!

· · ·

My father, bless his heart, used to say, "you're like a pestilent nematode worm that destroys wheat."

· · ·

Mike Bell gave me a wedgie so severe that sometimes after tacos I can still feel it.

· · ·

Up on the roof we were naked, Jordan and I, smoking a pipe packed with Mexican schwag.

· · ·

My parents bowled all Saturday long while we threw pool balls at each other in the bar.

· · ·

I remember the outfield grass, crickets, a balloon disappearing, and my father, drunk, yelling at the fence.

He pinned me to the floor, his fist on my neck, but I was running through fields.

. . .

I never fell into the frozen Greendale lake, though some part of me, evidently, is still there.

. . .

Those were the days, bright summers, knee-high socks, my sister inside giving the neighbor a hand job.

Note to Self
Have pity on all the pretty people walking dogs, they'll probably be dogs themselves next time around.

· · ·

When I heard she died I thought about everyone I didn't like and, suddenly, loved them all.

· · ·

Sun tells petunia, "open," and petunia tells hummingbird, "come in," and hummingbird tells me, "look, you bastard!"

· · ·

I've waited all day for the rain the woman on TV said would be here by now.

· · ·

All day the dogwood stood there, every now and then making some gesture I didn't really understand.

· · ·

I will stare hard until the last silver sketch of frost melts off the black imbricate rooftops.

· · ·

Here again on the couch, scribbling little nothings at the clouds, the city going on without me.

· · ·

I only had to do what I wanted to do but somehow could not even do that.

The best most of us do in life is fill well a six-foot hole in the ground.

. . .

I guess I'll have to go down and tell the pedophiles they can't get high here anymore.

. . .

Captain Meter Maid
This morning I noticed some super hero had thrown all the No Parking signs into the street.

. . .

I spent the morning watching the lavender bush and crabgrass entangled in a dance of mutual sabotage.

. . .

There's far too much ambition here, you can't be a simple bellboy without someone sneering "shame! shame!"

. . .

My most favorite things are all gone now, where I can make of them whatever I want.

. . .

Might as Well Be You
I guess someone has to go down and clean the feces off the neighbor's daughter's plastic tricycle.

. . .

I asked the oracle why we're supposed to ask questions of oracles and not icicles or basketballs.

I tried saying, singing, laughing, and even yelling, but the mountain never moved, the city stayed asleep.

. . .

I had a dream where I was told to use every word, even minesweeper, in a poem.

. . .

At night you wander through the old town's familiar streets, looking for lost, melting into the others.

. . .

I love the way the hydrangea flowers hang heavy in the sun out back of Jordan's garage.

. . .

We pretend the butterfly's lovely, a near perfect beauty, yet we barely take the time to look.

. . .

It's nice here once you realize you're alone with the clouds, and nothing people say is important.

. . .

I spent six months waiting (nothing better to do) for the irises to burst and flutter off.

. . .

The literati was terribly upset, but I couldn't feel anything except each of our bodies slowly decomposing.

. . .

One day—a day no different than the others—you'll realize that every single thing is singing.

A whole moon will shine in the night sky or clouded over shine somewhere lost behind it.

   . . .

The magpie on the split rail fence chirruped once and its whole body ruffled up with song.

   . . .

I interviewed in a soft sheer fabric made from fibrous pineapple leaves but didn't get the job.

   . . .

Yesterday But Not Today
I woke up early and remembered gladly that I hadn't had a single drink the night before.

   . . .

I was staring out the window when a breeze blew a thousand pink petals into my mouth.

   . . .

Best to sit beneath the willows and listen to what their branches have learned about this world.

   . . .

I will watch these trees until the light is gone; night doesn't fall, it dissolves us quietly.

   . . .

What did you do here? I tried to find the sacred things, I went looking every day.

   . . .

I looked everywhere I could think to look but all I seemed to find was my looking.

I went to the river to find a place to sit, and watch, and wait, to die.

. . .

The most essential prerequisite for making art (and living well) is accepting every answer as a proposition.

. . .

I walked down to the lake to leave me there, so I could visit now and then.

. . .

Who are these blossoming ones, here again to preach it, every year the same: "wake up, dumbshit!"

. . .

I spent the morning leaping from cloud to cloud, finding good in every god I came across.

. . .

I shoveled the snow off of the stairs, then watched the snow fall back onto the stairs.

. . .

I'm told "all things are beautiful" and I should just relax and let the carpet blossom out.

. . .

Once I realized I'd never get through to them I started trying to get through to me.

. . .

I walked out with her, looking hard at things, hoping to break into living with my eyes.

Maybe I'll just take a few days off and write about the traffic sounds or flower pots.

How can you wander if you won't allow for a world outside yourself? Kill yourself, and go.

I stared for hours at the plum tree blooming in the broken windshield of Jordan's mother's car.

Someday soon you'll be nearly dead and wish you could walk up to the park, just that.

The people leave in the morning, walking past the flowering quince as if it's not even there.

I was supposed to work, so I went to the park to eat some slow moving clouds.

To Do List
Cut the grass, weed the garden, get some beer, write a poem you would want to read.

The whole world, really, is a pearl, and we like hordes of spoiled swine move through it.

I should probably say something meaningful by the time I get to the end of this one.

It's nice to chat at strangers on the bus where there are so many kinds of ocean.

. . .

When I looked up, it was light, I'd somehow missed the greatest thing to happen that day.

. . .

I was dreaming, no, writing, no, sublime, I was in heaven, then lied my way through work.

. . .

Maybe I'll stop drinking and just turn brown or yellow, then let go of all my leaves.

. . .

Belly up to the bar, devour all you can until you can't eat another trainwreck or rose.

. . .

Don't speak to me of winter, every bare branch and parking lot is a field of flowers.

. . .

I rode my bike down to the lake to offer my complete devotion. Just that. Only that.

. . .

Live
In the stone a single word, in the clouds that word too, and everywhere else the same.

. . .

I think I might just go bird watching until this whole living business has run its course.

I dreamt that all the people walking cute little dogs were eaten by a swarm of chihuahuas.

. . .

I love the way the star-nosed mole interrogates the notion that somehow you and I are eccentric.

. . .

A cottonwood seed slowly drifted in the open window and effortlessly convinced the dog to swallow it.

. . .

I still think the little pig who built his house with straw was the wisest of all.

. . .

A pastern is that part of a horse's foot between the fetlock and hoof. Where are you?

. . .

Comfort Animal
Who knew that picking up dogshit is exactly what some people need to cure their anxiety issues.

. . .

The mountain cast its shadow over rolling hills of mallow spotted here and there with cattle grazing.

. . .

I would like to see, just once, a fire hydrant open up and pee on a dog.

Maybe They Don't Like Pink
For some reason the squirrels dug out all the petunias
we planted in the window box yesterday.

. . .

I love the mule at the Simpsons' farm and how it shits
with that *non chaloir* expression.

. . .

A crow with a baby bird in its beak, pecked at its skull,
then swallowed it whole.

. . .

The little dog with green ribbons makes a little puddle
on the floor when you smash it.

. . .

It took us nearly two weeks to plant the trees the beaver
gnawed down in a night.

. . .

I admit I was hoping all these people walking dogs would
contract a severe case of pinworms.

. . .

I realized in the zoo, sometimes it's fine to let a lion have
its way with you.

. . .

A mad frenzy of kinglets flew into the holly tree and at-
tacked its berries with perfect abolition.

I was watching the golden daffodils dancing in the breeze when the neighbor's horse devoured them all.

A bee landed on the stairs, rubbed its legs over its head and then (*bids*) flew off.

It strikes me that I always think of crows when some poet's mocking Stevens' poem about blackbirds.

It's nice the way everything seems to use everything else, bird and wasp and plant and sky.

We think the butterfly dazzles because the butterfly dazzles, but it does so because the darkness terrifies.

Skunk Love at First Sight
When I saw her I immediately ejected a foul-smelling oily liquid from the glands of my anus.

Proof That Dragons Exist
"Snapdragon" is derived from the flower's resemblance to "the mouths of dragons," not mouths of *imagined* dragons.

Two crows clasp their talons tight to the wires set bouncing when the electric bus walky-talkies by.

When the crocus opened the bees came buzzing in wildly
to plunder the open mouths of morning.

. . .

The earthquake shook the house, I ran out, panicked,
where I saw an ant hill quietly undisturbed.

. . .

I know it sounds superficial, but I'm profoundly moved
by the shifting cows on the opposite hill.

. . .

The dog left a damp ghost of shiver on the warm rocks
beside the ice cold river.

. . .

The quails skittered across the road, into the orchard:
we're all just little clowns avoiding our murderers.

. . .

We saw an otter in the river, or a coat I guess, plastic
bags around its neck.

. . .

Running
The dog runs out into the street, the car runs over it,
and the creek, and noses.

. . .

Do not presuppose that just because a hog is pink or very
round that it is ham.

The winter oak was circled by a steaming wreath of horses grazing as the freeway ordered by.

Despite the rain, I walked the dog to the park, and dug a hole, and buried it.

The life cycle of the newt flares red in its terrestrial stage so why then wouldn't we?

Where I Finally Found God
Traffic was so heavy it took me all morning to open the stomach of the runover squirrel.

Someday We'll Do That
I was sitting by the window when the starling crashed into the glass and just, well, died.

ART CRITICISM

At the gallery I found myself wishing I was in Central Park getting loaded with the drunks.

· · ·

I love the papal gauntness of El Greco's self-portrait beneath the Great Wall of China and grebe.

· · ·

When the arts become saturated with politics, they tend to tell it all and show virtually nothing.

· · ·

I confess I'll feel lucky if someday soon I have a gorgeous sculpted head like Georgia O'Keeffe.

· · ·

Monet
Better close your blue umbrella before the child is drowned by the poppies bleeding on the hill.

· · ·

It's true we have made some incredible things, but we ourselves will always be greater than them.

· · ·

I have found I mostly like to write ekphrastically when there aren't any works of art around.

· · ·

Legend says Nature herself killed Raphael because he painted more beautifully than she could hope to be.

· · ·

All I can think is every one of Degas' dancers has long ago rotted away to bone.

Art Fair
It's really too bad we've moved from landscape painting
to *en plein air* displays of abstract art.

. . .

I love the Dariagh Park painting of dunes and beach
grass, you could hide a body there.

. . .

Some boys, too, prefer to be Daphnes, not running away
but leafing out, reaching for the sky.

. . .

Satie was right about music, and like music, most things
are better when they're not really heard.

. . .

The marble spills over Apollo's waist, flows down, then
lifts as he slips into the laurel tree.

. . .

I have to admit I don't see what's so terrible about a
world with Caravaggio in it.

. . .

Horror Movie (Kiss)
I was kissing Debbie Harry when our lips grew together
and she turned suddenly into Andy Warhol.

. . .

Is Art progressing? Ammons: "someone may have writ-
ten music before or after Bach, but it wasn't necessary."

The doctor sighed, then: the bad news is you're dying, the good news is that's perfectly normal.

$\cdot \cdot \cdot$

I walked out and, attempting something great, was suddenly covered in a frenzy of ravenous fire ants.

$\cdot \cdot \cdot$

The essential value of any successful culture is the development of fear of some other culture.

A Brief Study of Clouds and Humans
Drift, dissolve, and then, disappear . . . if you look long enough you will find blackness behind them all.

$\cdot \cdot \cdot$

I accept you for who you are, but not for who you seem to think you are.

$\cdot \cdot \cdot$

There's really an overabundance of impracticality around, when you consider we're all soon burned or buried forever.

$\cdot \cdot \cdot$

Truth is a great and glorious thing, and sometimes shows us almost as much as what's false.

$\cdot \cdot \cdot$

I wonder if the dazzling maples are fully aware of the erosive machinations of autumn's dead breath.

Only after the sun rushed in did we realize we'd been somnambulists pitifully inept at living well.

. . .

When the diagnosis arrived, I marveled at all those years I'd spent worrying over nothing at all.

. . .

Life is fast, fleeting, a fall from sky to grave. Better have fun before forever finds you.

. . .

If you lie still enough at the bus stop, people will let you go ahead and die.

. . .

I made myself a beautiful building, and then I found some bricks to smash the windows with.

. . .

Nobody tells you beforehand: if you're lucky it will happen quickly, you might even lose your mind.

. . .

In the bar, Jordan shivers then flies out up to the wire where all her feathers iridesce.

. . .

When I don't allow myself enough time, I copy the ways of others, and forfeit my contribution.

. . .

I remember getting out of the car just as the rain came, thinking I would live forever.

You can play the game or question the rules, but you only get one turn. Ready? Go.

Every time it rains we think "oh fuck it's raining," not "I'm so lucky to be alive."

The blackberry vines are so bad you can't even hide a body without getting all scratched up.

We Were All Good People But
I remember how, on the train, no one wanted to sit where the Down's kids were standing.

All those dead people still living on video, dancing or singing or just drinking horchata in Tepic.

This morning the Rose of Sharon is blooming red, but the red rose is no longer sharing.

Isn't it funny how you never notice the funeral home, and then they cremate you in it?

The oracle was in poor taste, we thought, saying those dark things about what we'd all become.

When I finally realized what all of this was for, I was told I had to go.

. . .

Next to nothing I was really something, next to everything I wasn't much of anything at all.

. . .

Endless heavy rain, even the worms are out of their holes, but you are still in yours.

. . .

I will go too soon, I will write "I will go too soon . . ." and then I'll go.

. . .

We cannot hold a minute what's lovely, so we merely glimpse it then lie down in darkness.

. . .

I was drinking wine by the lake, but soon fell into the wine, and forgot the lake.

. . .

Even the French painter known for his scenes of festive gatherings has died! Even he! Even him!

. . .

I realized I was getting old when I wanted coffee more than sex from the tattooed barista.

. . .

Don't worry, the worst that will happen is that you'll be turned into some tree or flower.

Funny, when they tell you that you're dying you realize that you haven't really begun to live.

. . .

It's Unfortunate
When the sprinklers come on at some fancy house and you're trying to sleep in their garden.

. . .

We're all working hard every day on composing seventeen or so words that will decorate our headstones.

. . .

I realized too late that I was a charcoal drawing surrounded by a garish sea of color.

. . .

It never stopped raining in my grandmother's face, even when she died the rain just kept falling.

. . .

Why aren't we able to realize we're birds until we're worms remembering when once we were birds.

. . .

Okay fine this is all an illusion, but why is my illusion so full of medical bills?

. . .

And to think, instead of this I could've been the tenpin bowling champion of South Klackamas County.

Sometimes I find a wild wonder that is far worse than the drab grey of mild mediocre.

. . .

Outside, the bushes singing, the traffic singing, sycamores singing, and inside a dim hum chews our guts.

. . .

In the tavern we removed our skin and asked the bartender to just pour the alcohol in.

. . .

At the park the wind said, "see how I've been eroding you, and how you ignore it."

. . .

Who spent his life lost, a louse chewing on the pages of a labyrinthine dictionary of days.

. . .

Everyday's a daisy petal Death throws to the parking lot, she loves me, she loves me not.

. . .

I was late weeding the garden again this year, and again this year, the garden didn't care.

. . .

Mirror mirror on the wall, tell me something lovely false, or please tell me nothing at all.

A sponge bath's a bath but a bath you can't drown in, even though Jordan's mom did.

. . .

I waited all winter for the irises to bloom, then waited all spring for them to die.

. . .

A teaspoonful is all that a teaspoon can hold, how much, then, is a teaspoonful of limitless empty?

. . .

Where did all the romance go electrifying the drunken streets those warm summer nights now wasted, gone.

. . .

The weary old weathered bank we sledded down every winter now has a flashy new Taco Bell.

. . .

My sister called, which usually means someone's dead or dying, but this time it was just me.

You be the geranium and I'll be the hummingbird. And then, if you want, we can switch.

. . .

Okay, morning glory, I will pull you out again if that's what so thoroughly gets you off.

. . .

Before fall enflamed every leaf, the camellia blossoms opened up, saying "fuck me you pretty little birds!"

. . .

If an earthquake destroys our little town today, I guess I hope Jordan banged Claudio last night.

. . .

She says Pascal says what she says, which is why what she says must surely be true.

. . .

You will always be dear to me, picking cornflowers in the ditch where Indiana even seems lovely.

. . .

I will love you—all of you—like a quiet snowfall falling over every inch of you.

. . .

The words I wouldn't say, were the words I most needed to say, before that time ended.

. . .

Summer was an endless bore of drunkenness and sex, but rain this morning, at last this morning!

When I decided to trust her, I felt like a dazzled balloon shooting up into the sky.

. . .

I dreamt you were those bubbled gobs of spit bugs lined along my naked limbs, slowly eating me.

. . .

I remember how guilty you seemed, even though you just kept doing it, just kept destroying me.

. . .

I had the most amazing date with my dictionary last night. This morning the bedding was worsted.

. . .

You asked me my least favorite word, and all I could think of was you and Guadalcanal.

. . .

I was like a quiet little flowering shrub, when the swarm of bees came to ravage me.

. . .

Before Our Romantic Getaway; Or, Maybe We're Old
From the shower you said, "maybe we should bring the stack of New York Times Book Reviews?"

. . .

Sorry to be a bore but I think you left your herpes in my wife last night.

. . .

When I told my therapist my dominatrix was giving me an inferiority complex, she ended our sessions.

Those Were the Days

Don't you wish we were bored on that island again, driving around looking for something to do?

. . .

What things swell when the old singer sings that old song we knew when we were young.

. . .

Becoming intimate with someone only allows us a closer look at the lies we knowingly tell ourselves.

. . .

Since you left every cloud resembles you, so I just lie in the field all day, staring.

. . .

The news today is spring has come, the balconies full of bees buzzing round in wild geraniums.

. . .

I dreamt you were the moon and I had to watch you all night fucking the sea.

. . .

You asked me why I was miserable on such a lovely day, "darling, let me count the ways."

. . .

Jordan said, "let's go down to the field and look at the barn." "Look at the barn?" "Yes." "Okay."

. . .

I had a nice morning sitting at the window writing nasty little things about you and him.

Sorry, But
For a second the red branches of the sangu kaku made a
little fire in your eyes.

. . .

On a date overlooking the sea at sunset it's best not to
talk, and really anywhere else.

. . .

"Quiet," you said, and climbed onto me, and I felt no
need to say anything at all.

. . .

After Catullus
So I love, love, I love and hate, and this is a torture to
me, unbearable torture.

. . .

Aphid
I waited all winter for the daphne to bloom so I could
hatch and then get laid.

. . .

Franz Liszt is the most beautiful man in my dictionary,
and I've loved keeping him in there.

. . .

We're All the Same
Even the fuchsia in the window box is screaming, "come
stick your face in me while I'm alive!"

. . .

I cannot say grief, per se, for these nebulous clouds, no
clouds even, but an ill-defined hanging grey.

Happy Anniversary
We would like to not be doing this, you and I, so why then do we persist.

. . .

Mark Antony gave Cleopatra the entire library at Pergamum, please forgive me for only offering you these.

. . .

Pyracanthus
I climbed up your trellis to your window so I could serenade you with fire and thorn.

. . .

What's the use seducing when daisy petals know whether she loves me or she loves me not.

. . .

I was being Kurosawa when I asked you out, making films exactly the way I wanted to.

. . .

It's only March but already the engorged tips of the chestnut limbs are swelling up to flower.

. . .

Breakup
I thought I would just bury all your things with the dead hamsters Jordan forgot to feed.

. . .

Aubade
When morning stretched and broke, every lover left every lover's bed and wandered out into the cold.

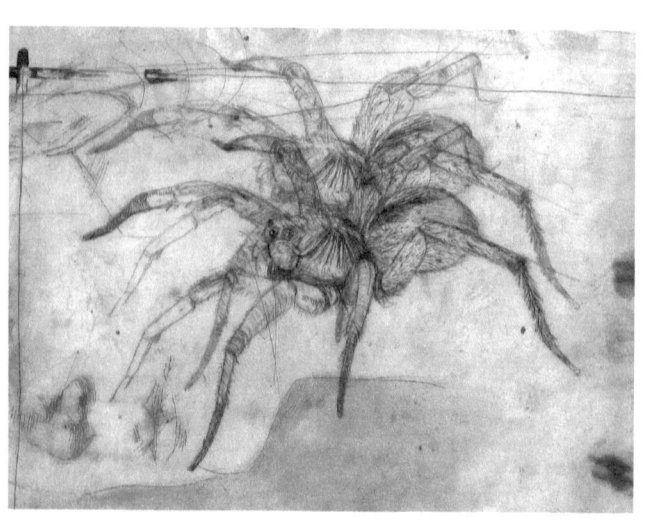

The moths in the park that night sputtered and spun like little laughs lighting up the dark.

· · ·

They frequently talked about other things besides cockroaches, but talking about cockroaches helped them best get along.

· · ·

During the fight, Jordan says, "stop complaining, haven't you figured out yet that all relationships are abusive."

· · ·

We woke early, a robin singing twined the air around us, it made of us a trellis.

· · ·

First Kiss
The hanging branches of the tamarisk tree fell over us as we hollowed out each other's skulls.

· · ·

Excuse
Jordan said the fog was so thick she mistakenly wound up sleeping with someone that wasn't me.

· · ·

It was love at last when you bent over and that perfect peony slipped from your ass.

So Happy Together
Jordan was on the couch across from me, reading and whispering, "I'm gonna break your fucking neck."

. . .

Matryoskha
Jordan gave me a bottle filled with several smaller bottles, and inside the last was her prick.

. . .

We nearly broke up over which was worse: "the lush greenness of flourishing vegetation," or, "crystalline verdancy."

. . .

Darling, Sweet, did you know there are more hairs on your back than stars in the sky?

. . .

Valentine
Here's a rotting rodent, a rat I found beneath the morning glory you've written on the wall.

. . .

After sex we have melba and smoosh old cakes in the humid cleft of Jordan's brown wagon.

. . .

Remember on the island, how we watched oyster catchers graze on the dark porous rocks bewildered with green.

Jordan says (rather rudely I think), "put the roses on my pussy and cover them with cum."

. . .

When I saw her passing, I smiled, and she smiled back, like a pile of dead leaves.

. . .

The hummingbird thrust its tongue into the depths of the camellia's damp billowing folds of sweet meringue.

. . .

Let's skip work today and walk around the city, just us, the others can go to hell.

. . .

Tomorrow's Valentine's Day so let's enjoy each other, soon we'll have to act like we're in love.

. . .

We waited on our islands for the space between us to disappear, for that myth of love.

. . .

I gave you a necklace of fragrant gardenias, and watched, and waited for the bees to come.

. . .

Someday my prince will come . . . in the form of a spring afternoon, and I'll be lazing, ready.

There's nothing wrong with registering to join political parties, some zoos are infinitely able to expand themselves.

· · ·

Most problems could be solved if we were willing to come to terms with the morning sky.

· · ·

Firecrackers sure, but not impulsive politicians quick to explode; the louder the mouth, the less it knows.

· · ·

We praise the ones we seek to build (or sustain) allegiances with, to the detriment of culture.

· · ·

The esteemed congressman proposed this morning the abolition of all motions in any way disagreeing with him.

· · ·

Why are we so often surprised that our governments lie when we lie so often to ourselves?

· · ·

We sometimes elect the most unattractive parts of us, as if to see if anything will change.

· · ·

The radicals on the courthouse lawn crying (only) "it's our turn to wear the masks of power!"

Time to wake up and tip the police cars over before they
put us all in jail.

It's unfortunate that so many liberals are bigger ass holes
than the conservative ass holes they condemn.

The sun has shone on many mockeries of justice, but why
then are we unable to see.

You can fight all your life to change the world, or you
can change your mind now.

I dreamt that all the Philistines were naked, little fishes
sucking at the source of their disdain.

Don't trifle with me about politics, not now, in April
when the magnolias are clearly in hysterics.

The Politician's Dilemma
The problem is to make them think there is a problem,
a problem much greater than themselves.

She says of the protest march passing our window:
"sounds like a one-man-band, but with 500 people."

Let's all play Roman statue and stand contraposto with long flowing chitons and our swollen heads removed.

. . .

It's best to go for a walk in the rain and let it wash your politics away.

. . .

Dear Mom
Thanks for watching the cat while Jordan and I dropped shitbags outside the Trump Tower revolving doors.

. . .

Coincidence
I threw the whiffle ball and when you hit it the president tweeted "I'm a talking donkey."

. . .

We like to think we own our bodies, but no idea inside our heads belongs to us.

. . .

Power is so attractive that the potential of having it ourselves keeps our oppressors securely in office.

. . .

It was an extraordinary day, hydrangeas blooming in the neighbor's garden, no one fighting over the election.

. . .

Heist
The car sped away with a backseat full of Donald Trump's panties. Good luck selling those!

Mike Pence is living proof that some people always seem to have that "dick-in-the-headlights" look about them.

· · ·

The Gravity of the Situation
Freedom would be nice, but we are like kites the moon holds in its bloody little hands.

· · ·

How speak to the wind when *he* is in office and every orifice is full of him.

· · ·

Against Interpretation
Jordan had a dream that Trump was blowing her and she was shooting razorblades into his mouth.

· · ·

The stubborn refusal to relinquish irrationally optimistic views comes across as the most cynical form of pessimism?

· · ·

It struck me that, in a breeze, a maple tree expresses contrary notions; why then, don't you?

· · ·

Perverse this constant arguing, when life's just a fog; we all think only what others have thought.

· · ·

What's the use of constructing categories or manufacturing divisions from which to hurl insults. Look: it's snowing.

What I Heard
Take this willow branch, this clear sky and this quiet
pasture, and now sing me something . . . sing.

. . .

Blurb
This truly remarkable poet of unmistakably lineated lan-
guage has chosen a delightful cover image for their book.

. . .

Yesterday I wrote the most lovely poem that's turned
into the most horrid thing I've ever seen.

. . .

I guess I'm kind of looking forward to the day when ev-
eryone "writing" erasures is erased away.

. . .

Said Field to Breeze
You must be terribly dissatisfied moving all these flow-
ers about but never really able to grab on.

. . .

On shore a glaucous gull reads a Field Guide to Bald Fat
Poets of the Pacific Northwest.

. . .

It's fine to talk to ghosts, to sing them little songs or put
flowers in their eyes.

. . .

Even if haiku makes you vomit, you have to admit it
solves the problem of pleonastic writing.

I've tried but it doesn't seem these alchemies are working; I haven't even grown a mosquito wing.

. . .

A stone is concreted earth or mineral matter; a poem is concreted musical sentiment in words.

. . .

Ask Yourself
What is this clay pot I've bore? Is it lovely wild enough and who is it for?

. . .

For me, form is a way of holding onto life, a crudité of morning, noon, and night.

. . .

If I imagine a voice, and write what it's said, am I transcribing mind, body, or spirit?

. . .

You can't move to Malibu with poetry, but you can build a dazzling house in the clouds.

. . .

I can't stand constraint based poetry, the counterintuitive sense of limitless freedom makes me feel insufferably claustrophobic.

. . .

By the time my book came out, the city was filled to choking with everyone else's book.

What if you just said, I feel like life is slipping away and I can't comprehend that.

. . .

I knew you once, the thousandth time, before you slipped away to hide again, the thousandth time.

We think we sing, but no one sings; it's the song that sings us, until it stops.

. . .

I got a call today from Jordan, whose poems are absolutely horrible but who's really lovely herself.

. . .

"Scansion" is derived from Latin, "to climb," as if the poetic line could lead us to heaven.

. . .

I dreamt Joanne Kyger turned into a flower pot from which I sprung as a dry bouquet.

Someday I'll think to figure out what all this singing's about, but not now, please not now!

. . .

Yeats, too, wrote a book about wind and reeds and hoped he'd become the things he said.

. . .

Sometimes very simple facts appear, and you devote yourself to singing them, but still they get misheard.

The Instagram poet was blowing up, so I ran for cover
. . . as far away as I could.

. . .

When I read Richard Hugo I write horribly lachrymose
poems about Butte, towering Buicks and old blondes.

. . .

Let's go now, can you hear it? The pear, the core, the hot
thrill of being alive.

. . .

To My Daughter
If I ever write poems as bad as Raymond Carver, please
just tie me to a rowboat and push me out to sea.

. . .

I love the way the morning garbage trucks' lurching and
clanging open jaws aspire to imitate birdsong.

. . .

Some of the coffee in the sentence, "Jordan drank some
of the coffee," Jordan actually did drink.

. . .

Walking under an enormous cherry tree I said, "cherry
tree," but it said nothing, just stood there.

. . .

I absolutely love the word, "splish," and certainly con-
sider it more than enough for taking a bath.

Keats
Here lies one whose name was writ in Whoopiecushions,
who had a clown nose for every occasion.

Like All of Us
I like to think I'm one who is immune from slipping into
affected wisdoms and saccharine cliché.

I thought, "I will say something clear and forceful," but
when I spoke: more of the same.

Concentration is a kind of levitation, and when you're
in the clouds it's easy to love indiscriminately.

How was I to know my lovely song sounded as if my
mouth was full of snow.

It's difficult to write a decent poem about the moon, as
the moon itself is a poem.

She Can't Stand Titles Like This
Every time I write something fantastic it flutters off like
an io moth and then just dies.

Grant Application
Dear Distinguished, forgive me this bluntness, but will
you please put your money where my mouth is.

How does this machine work? Do I put the flowers here, or subtly, let them just disappear?

. . .

She said, "I don't get your poems. They sound like falling leaves." Okay, I thought, that's enough.

. . .

I was thinking about the avant-garde and how it fragments or even discontinues just when you least.

. . .

Moon Colony
The word moon isn't, of course, the moon, but a magical spell where we can live forever.

. . .

What if, all this time, the birds singing in the neighbor's hedge were aspiring to imitate *us*?

. . .

It's too bad so many have parodied Stevens' blackbird poem and so few have actually read it.

. . .

1: I'm so glad counting in poetry is out of fashion. 2: I guess it was a 90s thing.

. . .

What did you do here? I read poems to fence posts, I tried to wake them up.

Do we really need to mention that in all this nothingness a tiny leaf bedazzles the mind.

. . .

Language is everywhere around us, waiting to write itself through us, for us to let it sing.

. . .

Even the most beautiful writers say they're unable to feel deeply what beauty they're able to write.

. . .

Poem be my wage, my work and my reward, both my prison and my escape from prison.

. . .

Hey Daddy
At the poetry reading the poets were serving bowl after bowl of Plath, Sexton, and Robert Lowell.

. . .

Hoping to transcend the sentimentality of my earlier work, I thought I'd just do this: Help me!

. . .

When the sun suddenly appeared, I thought, "now that marks the arrival of a major visionary poet."

. . .

For Some of Us It's More Difficult
Unlike Berryman, my father never killed himself, I wasn't blessed with easy entries to alcohol and dream-songs.

Sometimes it seems every poem is a search for light, no matter how faint, in insufferable darkness.

   . . .

Everyone writes poetry now, which is just wonderful, except for the fact that everyone writes poetry now.

   . . .

Jordan says that every poem, even the briefest, exacts a life, and then at the end: death.

   . . .

Perhaps the lyre that Sappho played was just missing a string or two, and that's why her

   . . .

I tried to write something that would lift us all out of this filthy sack of worry.

   . . .

How To Catch a Fish
Write your hands fast into the stream, or slow, no need of catching where all fish go.

   . . .

Poetry Lesson
The only difference between horses and unicorns is a single horn; so add a horn, dumb ass.

   . . .

I sat down near the autumn oak to write simply, "I sat down near the autumn oak."

There's no need to worry much over what poems intend to say, what clouds intend to say.

. . .

Is it true that in Yeats' time, life and death were just rhyme after rhyme after rhyme?

. . .

The Court Poets' Defense
We weren't exactly out to storm the castle walls, but to regard them as evening slipped away.

. . .

Yeats obviously built his cabin "of clay and wattles made" with the second little pig in mind.

. . .

Is that all you want from poetry, to just predictably address the socio-political events of the day.

. . .

At least literary critics have stopped using the phrase, "full disclosure," and are now again unapologetically favoritist.

. . .

I wrote hard, with intense focus, the beautiful lines that rang and rang and then betrayed me.

Sure, some of us couldn't understand what the others were saying, but most weren't listening at all.

* * *

At the reading there were thirty readers (thirty readers!), thirty readers hearing only one voice: their own.

* * *

I picked up the old poet's self-published book—his fifty-sixth collection—aptly titled *Surely Not Another One*.

* * *

Some of us were trying to get to the top, while others were still building the thing.

* * *

Some of us jumped off before we were even finished, that's how romantic we proved to be.

* * *

So many poets these days sticking their confessions in everyone's mouth, as if we hadn't already eaten.

* * *

I dreamt I swung a scythe and the skyscrapers along the lake fell one by one by . . .

* * *

What's the use of language if everyone's chattering like mad parrots in the Norfolk pines at dusk?

It's obvious your manifesto makes manifest certain said truths you claim to find clearly evident for yourself.

. . .

So many of us shout, loudly ranting, but you cannot address the silence in us with shouts.

DEAR GOD

They say I mistook the love of god for a septic field, but there were daisies everywhere.

. . .

The grasses growing above the dunes were glowing green, chartreuse, we walked for days and days and.

. . .

I saw some people far away, they were minuscule, when they died I couldn't grasp the enormity.

. . .

When the bridge emerged from the fog we all wondered if we had made it suddenly appear.

. . .

Why is it we are so aware of living when we are waiting alone for a train.

. . .

I said "here, I will give my life to you," and you received me without a sound.

. . .

I don't like the word "cremate" for what they do to us, sounds like a coffee condiment.

. . .

Strange we have to learn the old lessons again and again: wake up, smell the lemons, listen.

. . .

I walked out into the sunlit field where you were lolling and picked a bucketful of you.

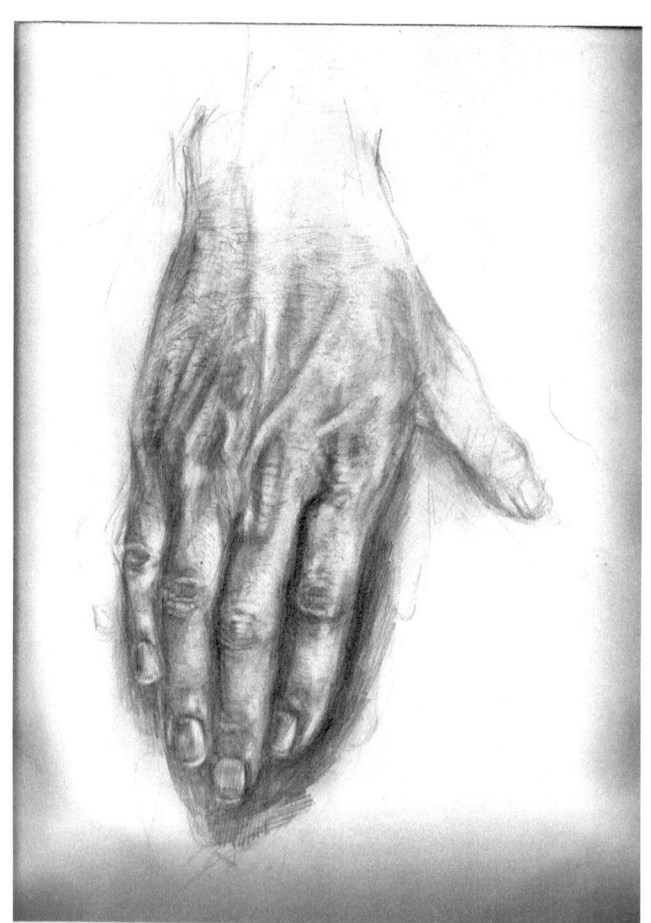

What is it really, that is so difficult? To wander here awhile, to die just once forever.

. . .

I'm enjoying all the things I haven't forgotten yet, even the terrible things I can't quite forget.

. . .

I laid beneath the live oak tree all day listening, searching the sky but you wouldn't speak.

. . .

Opening the door I nearly fell, the petunias were so vibrant bright magenta spilling from the windowbox.

. . .

Someone in the souped-up car passing us, yelled, "go fuck a biscuit pan!" and then sped off.

. . .

I wouldn't mind an ecclesiastical pardon, just not today, not while there's so much sugar lying around.

. . .

Narcissus
I was noticing the way the water warps a reflection, I wasn't looking at me at all.

. . .

I'll follow you into the forest, but not the barn. I won't go in there with you.

Please help me carry my carcass across this bog of briars, it will only take a second.

. . .

How miserable this life can be, and how we clown around, drunk either on bibles or beer.

. . .

What will fall when I fall, and fill the puddles in the alley so murky and bottomless.

. . .

I've tried to be as light as kerria for you, and sometimes drew a smile or two.

. . .

If the geranium makes it through the winter I'm giving up all these ridiculous notions of mortality.

. . .

All I really wanted to do was use the phrase "drowning in light" when I mentioned you.

. . .

Veronica
The wafers are delicious in the little village where they found the handkerchief impressed with Jordan's face.

. . .

Every morning I'm amazed by the blue light azure marinade, how nobody seems to drown in it.

Something in the way those leaves fell made me think
we'd be okay; I know it's ridiculous.

Save me from the others and deliver me to trembling
alpine heather blooming quiet by the lake.

I stood in the sun at the gates to the mission, hoping
they'd never allow me inside.

After the neighbor's wedding party, the garbage was
strewn and lovely; all the useless things are mine.

I had a dream that everyone's xmas lights turned to
moths, and every moth to quiet humility.

We know where yellow snow comes from, but where
these yellow clouds and all the yellow flowers?

JOGGERS

All the joggers jogging down the street with earbuds in
I wonder if you can eat them.

· · ·

The joggers passed and I went running after them yelling
"give me back my beautiful baby boy!"

· · ·

I'll leave too because I hear lakewater lapping, Yeats
wasn't the only one who liked to runaway.

· · ·

I wonder if there's a hole, something like a landfill, that
all the joggers eventually fall into.

· · ·

This morning some joggers found a corpse beneath the
gingko tree we sometimes hang our hammock in.

· · ·

It rained for several weeks before the remains in the
cemetery bubbled up and ran quietly away.

· · ·

I watched a hawk light down from the roof and scream-
ing rip open the fit jogger's face.

· · ·

The bus never came so I hopped on one of those joggers
that just kept running by.

· · ·

When the joggers got to my window I yelled, "soon your
legs will rot off you bastards!"

I was happy to see the joggers jogging and the lions chasing them down and devouring them.

. . .

Earlier came a jogger so portly, all the puddles in all the potholes giggled as he passed.

. . .

This morning a thin jogger with a tiny yellow dog ran straight into a blue Dodge van.

. . .

The old lady on the corner yells out the window "jogging will make you a beautiful corpse!"

. . .

The joggers have all come out to terrorize the morning streets, and heavy clouds cover the sky.

. . .

We were so irate because several joggers just ran past even though Jordan was obviously giving birth.

. . .

This morning some joggers ran past and when they did the neighbor's garbage can ran after them.

. . .

I was watching when the jogger unhorsed with a malefic splat and a sobbing bag of oats.

. . .

All day the joggers ran bouncing past the vinaceous leaves of the maple heavy with Oregon juncos.

At least when it storms the joggers don't plague the side-walks and parks with their horrible fitness.

. . .

On every single sidewalk this morning several species of stinging ant spilled from every jogger's sweat-soaked skin.

. . .

I love the varied choreographies of jogger's limbs past the neighbor's fir trees in the morning sun.

One problem with sport fishermen is that they don't seem to realize they're already teeming with fish.

. . .

The collective mind evidently leads to what's most mundane, the dumbest peg finds (and defines) the (w)hole.

. . .

The Problem with Other People
I wish you'd just see me for who I imagine myself to be instead of this disaster.

. . .

Why do we truck away all the lovely leaves and dump them in a hole in Kent.

. . .

All these self-righteous people do indeed see very clearly, but only the things that they can see.

. . .

What's the use of hiking up a mountain when you can just sit and stare at it.

. . .

In the dog park every dog has a man or woman, and every phone has one too.

. . .

The party was mealy with the endlessly hackneyed political slogans of the radical this, the self-righteous that.

The tourists are packed into Cannery Row, and drink until they puke their clams and marinated escargot.

. . .

In the quiet city park, I shot my gun, and up flew a hundred thousand homeless fathers.

. . .

I'll also like it when the others are gone, and we can just be quiet and read.

. . .

The mother of one's wife or husband is best kept in a brown paper bag or gamelan.

. . .

Some tulips distract from the weeds growing around them, some are pretty and have no sinister design.

. . .

Gentrification
The three of them were wearing wetsuits—father, mother, child—and drinking coffee at Starbucks, in wetsuits.

. . .

If you drop your phone and go outside, there are things in the garden that can help.

. . .

It's amazing how we'll forgive the pervert even his exposed prick if it's a beautiful spring day.

Ambition is a bag of lack, besides, who wants to be the queen of roller coaster rides?

. . .

It's embarrassing how garish purple pink the sunrise and the lengths we go to avoid seeing it.

. . .

Why is it that we tend to lock ourselves in cages even as we set us free?

. . .

If Narcissus had turned into skunk cabbage instead of a daffodil maybe there'd be fewer narcissists today.

. . .

Everyone knows the reason we move around so much is so no one will notice we're dying.

. . .

Sometimes in the mall the people are so affected I feel like I'm on the planet Douchebag.

. . .

Are we ourselves the dolls we ourselves wed to other dolls? Is the whole world playing dress-up?

. . .

More stars in the sky or more turtle photo ops at the Bethesda fountain in Central Park?

. . .

There's no mirror that doesn't contort, we're all in the funhouse, most of us build our own.

Not until I lost my phone, did I call everyone to get in touch, to say hello.

　　　. . .

Dear Football Fans
Though it's hard to swallow, erectile dysfunction is a natural phenomenon highly beneficial to the human race.

　　　. . .

Don't assume the others climbing the mountain are actually there and not on some other distant hill.

　　　. . .

What's the use of doing all the things we do if soon we'll just forget them anyway.

　　　. . .

It's odd the way a quiet evening will quickly collapse into ruin with a single thoughtless remark.

　　　. . .

Don't judge a cover by its book, else you won't be able to look at anyone's face.

　　　. . .

The new "intellectuals" compete to see who can hang the most people in a single, vitriolic rant.

　　　. . .

We call strong those insecure people whom we can plainly see desperately need to be called strong.

It's funny how we all expect to die like a wise monk or gentle sheep simply sleeping.

. . .

Some of us wake up to find we've been dreaming, some of us just won't stop sleeping.

. . .

People work all their lives to be happy even though being happy's really nothing much at all.

. . .

Those who confess always ask us to believe that their confessions are for someone other than themselves.

. . .

Funny how we gather together, happy to have the company, all of us going our separate ways.

I do love Jordan but her dick has been in more mouths than a Michael Jackson song.

Anton von Leuwenhoek
What I need is another day just lounging, just sitting on the leeboard formulating descriptions of spermatozoa.

Reading Heraclitus Beside the Nisqually
All morning the river's laugh disturbed the forest's quiet, a constant spilling cataract stepping in the book.

Oscar Wilde dressed garish from foot to mouth, even his tepid outfits resembled a Raphaelesque Renaissance couch.

Someday maybe even I can be as strong as Oprah Winfrey, giving them all what they want.

John Kennedy Toole
I drove to Biloxi and found a place to idle the car so I could stop this.

In the dream, Neal Hamburger just came out and said that Tony Clifton was his baby daddy.

I heard you say that Evelyn Waugh looked like a frightened possum, headlights in his pinhole eyes.

. . .

John Wayne loved leather so much they replaced his skin with it, a wrinkled sack of it.

. . .

The Kardashians
I bet it's strange to walk around with flowers up your ass and everyone grabbing after them.

. . .

Thyestes unknowingly ate the flesh of his own sons and then, knowing, wept, wept only in knowing.

. . .

Jordan said, "when you're referring to my penis please use 'terra firma' and not 'Justin Bieber.' Thanks."

. . .

The dahlias nod on the edge of the park, and we search them for some resemblance of us.

. . .

Messiah
George Frederick Handel's picture in my dictionary is proof that evolution still has some work to do.

. . .

Schuyler summing up his time as Creative Writing Professor: "Holy fuck the reams of shit I've read!"

Jordan once proposed that Roethke and Hugo shared the same body, the one Alfred Hitchcock threw away.

Henrik Ibsen's barbarous herd of cattle must've cut his beard to where their necks just couldn't stretch.

The reading held only fifty people, but a hundred of them were dreaming of fucking Jericho Brown.

This morning I was reading when the sun harried in, aggressive as the beard of John Berryman.

To give praise to a machine with a rotating blade for cutting grass makes Jerry Jones hard.

I'm getting close to fifty and lately I've been feeling about as bad as Somerset Maugham looks.

DESIRE

The waves crashed, eager all day, and all day I was unable to give what they wanted.

. . .

I stared long at the fractured sculpture of Ceres, waiting for the present world to fade away.

. . .

This one's not for you, it's for another part of you, the part that you dissolve into.

. . .

I was thinking I might go out and pull a cloud down or strangle a garbage truck.

. . .

Summer longs for autumn, autumn for winter, winter for spring, and spring? spring needs nothing at all.

. . .

Will I ever write or recite a line that hangs like the purple petunias twine and hang?

. . .

What the River Said
I waited all night for the moon to fall into my mouth, and then I swallowed it.

. . .

All I ever wanted to do was be the ground beneath my feet, and the sky above.

My entire life has been a desperate attempt to trick into song the way that morning begins.

. . .

I tried to jump up and join the clouds but could only stay there for an instant.

. . .

Fog
Hungry, I ate a thick coast of trees then ran around giddy in the autumn, Aberdeen rain.

. . .

I bent over and buried my face deep into the ovary of an Elizabeth Cady Stanton rose.

. . .

The dream in me walked for years like a heron hunting a grassy marsh but catching nothing.

. . .

I sat and watched the ants for hours, wishing I could crawl into the crack with them.

. . .

I opened up my flower petals and let the rain pour in, desperate for (even) imagined feeling.

. . .

"No fish?" you said, what do you mean, no fish? can't you see I'm catching the river.

. . .

I stared at the crow on the lawn but no length of looking let me see it.

In the lovely dream I was a storm drain, and some white camellias filled up my mouth.

I remember being so hungry we ravaged the dirt and grass beneath the bare winter apple tree.

I just wanted to make sure we ate a lawn at least once before we wandered off.

What I need is just one more early morning silence breaking into noisome vivant garbage truck song.

When I lay down with my cigarette in the puddle of gasoline, life began its brilliant blossoming.

In the creek the salmon work day after day just to reach another pool mere yards away.

All night in the streets and alleys I yelled at the moon but it never yelled back.

I begged and groveled at the feet of flowers to show me just once how to bloom.

My whole life trying to be as simple and careless as loosestrife waving in the evening breeze.

Walking through the marsh I asked only that my open
eyes open more, and more, then, more.

. . .

Maybe someday I will be a French botanist, and you will
name a hapless shrub after me.

. . .

My eyes like gravestones always looking down, but I will
dance wild in clouds now I swear.

. . .

I know this is taxing, please forgive me, I only mean song
wildly reaching out to you.

Keats said poetry should surprise by a "fine excess,"
something like a lovely little daffodil . . . that retches.

· · ·

Colette
It's only because other things fly—we have seen them
do it!—that we ourselves desire wings.

· · ·

Ammons
Release us from mental prisons into the actual fact, the
mere occurrence—the touched, tasted, heard, seen.

· · ·

Baudelaire
The study of beauty is a duel in which the artist shrieks
with terror before being overcome.

· · ·

Hejinian
As for those of us who like to be astonished, thicken the
eggs in a bath, Marie!

· · ·

Ammons
In art we do not run after random moments, we select
and create the moment occurring forever.

· · ·

Berryman (Dream Song 187)
The terrible truth: it is a true error to marry with poets
or to be by them.

Yeats
Pluck till time is done the silver apples of the moon the golden apples of the sun.

Kyger
Finally it's out the door and down the trail where the lovely breach draws me into her.

Berryman says, "mutter we all must as well as we can," monkey mouths in a monkey tower.

La Rochefoucauld says, "some people are like popular songs that you only sing for a short time."

Levertov
The low cloud at the far end of the cattle field hanging near the cottonwood, nothing else.

All night it rained and all day and then all night and all day it rained again.

. . .

How is it this one moment, somehow, is worth everything I've done? Open window, chill morning breeze.

. . .

I hung my hammock from the gingko tree and waited for the gingko dreams to devour me.

. . .

The best thing about a hot August day is the thought of a mist damp February beach.

. . .

I Sometimes Sleep There
The alley behind The Booklouse Saloon has deep doorways, nice evening light, and very few blood stains.

. . .

You only really know a city when you realize everything you've heard about it is absolutely false.

. . .

Someday soon you'll collapse and people will stare, or ignore you, acting like they don't really understand.

. . .

This morning I went down to the marsh to watch the birdwatchers frighten off the native birds.

Broken glass tastes best before standing in rose colored puddles that fill up your chest-high rubber waders.

. . .

We were eating sorrel by the creek when Jordan said, "I think the dog peed on these."

. . .

I hid behind the sweet gum waiting to throw dead rats at the numbnuts on their phones.

. . .

I Love Jordan
Jordan leapt onto the desk and then let loose a walloping pregnancy of happy baby fucking noises.

. . .

No one ever says "Darling let's honeymoon with the inbreds hunting muskie just south of Green Bay."

. . .

Dear Hippopotamus, you are the fattest most beautiful weirdo I've ever wanted to sit on my face.

. . .

It's prudent to judge any venture on whether or not it will lead to a picnic table.

. . .

I like to think my friends never die, they're just always at a different bar than me.

The little lovely child was swept quick out to sea, terror fading, slowly giving way to resignation.

. . .

From the privet hedge, Jordan can masturbate in peace to all the kindergarten moms in yoga pants.

. . .

The best hedges for sleeping in are osmanthus, their sweet scent dribbling down nearly all night long.

. . .

I learned well once that fire ants prefer not to have their nests covered with sleeping bags.

. . .

I watched her drift out into the bay, a softly glowing child just this side of drowning.

. . .

It was spring and the streets were all plum blossoms and Mardi Gras beads strangling our necks.

. . .

You may think you're living a long meaningful life, but fingernails and hair live longer than you.

. . .

It seems obvious that the most beautiful things always end with someone lovely drowning in a lake.

Oh Yay They're Here!
She was laying carpet when the postman brought the
butterfly wings she'd ordered from the Happy Store.

. . .

Just ahead of the rainstorm, the dandelions stretched
themselves slightly to say "listen, can you smell it?"

. . .

I thought that it had stopped raining but realized the
rain had just turned to grey skin.

. . .

If unicorns are mythical creatures, well then how does
Jordan keep pulling them out of her ass.

. . .

The school bus was gorgeous marigold orange, though
it never grew again after careening into the canal.

. . .

It was so light, so gorgeous swimming after her, in that
undertow before we both disappeared.

. . .

The sandwich board outside the restaurant in southern
Mississippi advertised "Mama's grits and greens in Bib-
lical proportions."

. . .

The pear trees opened today and several trucks and
busses just drove right off the Brooklyn Bridge.

A baby, wearing only diapers, fell out the window and down into the pavement's wide open arms.

When Jordan says, rather crudely, "the Museum of Natural History is huge," what she means is big-boned.

Thaumaturgy is the art of making miracles, the first of which is the correct spelling of thaumaturgy.

The thing about a public toilet is, once you've used it, Jordan goes bowling in red macramé.

When they drained the muddy pond, they found a thousand toads croaking around the murdered boy's body.

Passing The Plaza Hotel with the pleasant thought, "at least I'll never have to go in *there*."

The top hat sang like a bird and then flew off, alive with the old magician's head.

I opened my grandma's pillbox so she and I could smoke a blunt together and watch TV.

Several crows were terrorizing a limp toupee while an old bald man looked on from his wheelchair.

As we left the grocery, Jordan pushed a canary melon up my ass, "to check the air."

. . .

We were drinking coffee in the square when the car came and bodies flew, like dress dummies.

. . .

This life will be forgotten so completely not the least scratch of any scribbling hand will remain.

. . .

The sky was quiet, a gentle birdsong blue, when Jordan dropped a dead rat at my feet.

Monkeysteps
Stretching long, I lifted up to see above the tall grasses, and leaning forward failed to fall.

. . .

It's funny how we think we're more than just some simple riverweeds swaying in a filthy creek.

. . .

Disproving the Existence of God
Why would we invent a god if god already existed? There wouldn't be any need for Him.

. . .

I had a dream that all my Facebook friends not only "liked" me but actually liked me.

. . .

When the sun came out, I was one fleck or flake on one globe, in one universe.

. . .

It happened again, one of them died and said, "I missed it," sky suddenly dark, night begun.

. . .

Playing billiards in Hawaii is the closest any of us will ever get to being Greek Gods.

. . .

So many yell out in certainty the answers to near insolvable entanglements, and then just stop thinking.

All night lying in bed dreaming of the dark terrible things the dark terrible night can do.

The heart can see what the head cannot, so the head tries to tear out the heart.

I woke before the others, so I could lift again the knowledge that I'd have to die.

Funny how we distract ourselves in order to deal with life, yet cannot bear all the distractions.

Who doesn't enjoy walking and meditating, but you can't stop, otherwise you go straight back to hell.

If I told you everything there is to know, would you still wonder what I'd left out?

Nature is, of course, very beautiful, nearly perfect: its only flaw is that *we* didn't do it.

Someday something like a wooly mammoth will say dreamily of us, "wow, those things must've been cool."

Snow will make a child of the oldest among us, but rain will age even the unborn.

Just when I realized I was alive and so lucky to be that way, that realization ended.

. . .

A Glimpse of the Future
It was as if I was flying, butterfly-like, when I had that premonition of darkness to come.

. . .

Our strongest influences are usually from those things in absentia, after all, what's really here with us?

. . .

Self-hatred is an organ we all have in common, we all must forgive before we can love.

. . .

I agree with Ammons: we're monkeys scratching our heads and asses and dumb with joy and tragedy.

The little blue Jetta (the large white neighbor drives)
sits alone beneath a macklemore of chattering starlings.

. . .

We think the kookaburra laughs (*Dacelo gigas*), but really,
maybe it just wants to fuck our ears.

. . .

The crow cawed then flew across the street, landed on
the wire, cawed again, the same thing.

. . .

A rain will beat down on a corrugated roof, but it will
never beat down on moss.

. . .

In the dream I was awake and dreaming of the lakeshore
where we slept beneath the cottonwoods.

. . .

Swan Song
The beautiful legendary song sung only once by a swan
in its lifetime, sung as it's dying.

. . .

Scarecrow / Sparrows
A gang of them fluttered in and covered Jordan standing
in the blue dim before day began.

. . .

The lorikeet didn't sing so loud when I put it in the
neighbor's shiny red Porsche.

The robin sings hours before the sun rises, until the sun rises saying, "okay okay, you win."

. . .

When the sun hit the maple tree, all the pretty sparrows said to me, "wake up, asshole!"

. . .

The flicker aspires to imitate Phillip Glass, and also to wave and wavelet overlapping the corrugate shore.

. . .

The truth is, I put the first robinsong of morning in the garbage truck where it belongs.

. . .

The robin (again!) this morning, on the wire in the dark dusk singing, something wild with meaning.

. . .

The skylark is "noted for singing while flying," a kind of ornithological version of drinking and driving.

. . .

The creek grackles and rills, a shrift palimpsest hum when the heron lifts, belches and vomits broth.

. . .

The rail rose rambled and rose around the rail twining its tiny thorns and small white words.

Sorry But It Froze
The winter wren landed on the iron rail and shouted out
"where the fuck is my geranium!"

. . .

Bare now, and dry, the summer fields we walked in all
spring, daisies and carrot flowers gathering.

. . .

I dreamt I was sailing along a calm lagoon on your
grandma's couch with the rose festoon.

. . .

When the wave receded the sandpipers ran fast to the
sea singing "ooh loot pools of it!"

. . .

The new Japanese maple leaves are now unloosed, bright
where the new morning light turns them chartreuse.

. . .

I don't really think my small intestines have said all the
things you claim to have heard.

. . .

A titmouse can be a chickadee but cannot sing very long
in a jar, plastic or glass.

. . .

A robin is a token symbolizing dusk, dawn, and also like
us, a living thing nearly gone.

Upriver the loud chatter of kingfisher and merganser
near out-babbled the raucous rilling of the rapid stream.

. . .

The clouds this morning hung low, hiding a few crows,
black as boots lost in the snow.

. . .

I like birds because they use simple words like macadam
and Visigoth, porcupine and yellow rubber ocelots.

. . .

If we knew exactly what the crow was saying, we might
never walk down this street again.

. . .

This morning the birds were singing, "leave me weary
pleasingly," but the garbage truck sang "NOT NOW!"

. . .

How much wood could a whistle pig chuck if a wood
pussy could be called a skunk?

. . .

If I could sing like these summer evening summer robins
I'd never need to write another word.

. . .

It's Odd
Some days the best thing that ever happens is hearing
"hedgehog" as if for the first time.

A raucous scree of juncos fluttered through the winter sweet gum, then fast into my open mouth.

. . .

All my poems flew in a flurry of phoneme and fireweed through the hole in my skull.

. . .

When morning light spread across the tops of the ficus trees, a thousand crows called "caw cacophony."

. . .

I love how we like to think that birds are singing to us, as if we mattered.

. . .

In the marsh the red-winged blackbirds trilling call out to others but I never hear my name.

. . .

Gargling helps a sore throat but soaring won't help you gargle or find god quicker than walking.

. . .

The crow caws with all its body, yet all my body only just barely begins to hear.

. . .

Listen!, there it is again, the tulips and the sound they make when the sunlight opens them.

. . .

All my life for this, fox sparrow calling from the linden tree, "this is all there is."

What is the custom here in your city? Can I shove the leaf blower up your ass?

Let's stay here, in Philadelphia, where no one knows us at all, where we can be invisible.

Jordan said New Orleans is a zydeco band with red garters hanging off the balconies sniffing coke.

Oh for a—I wouldn't say beaker full but yes, certainly— bucket full of the warm south.

Feel Like I've Died and Gone to Pittsburgh
The first spring sunlight spilled onto us like molten iron into the molds of a pig bed.

I'm still hoping one day I too can be the first to fly solo over the Atlantic.

St. Claude and Louisa
We walked through the streets alive with cockroaches scattering from the discarded heels of uneaten po' boys.

Let's build a park in place of Lake Shore Drive, the Age of the Automobile finally done.

Remember how we died on the beach in Belize, the cream-thick quiet waves, the women selling litchis.

· · ·

Mardis Gras
I must've received a thousand beads but everytime I showed my tits the bastards wanted a refund.

THIS, THEY SAY, WILL HAPPEN

As you get older a year passes more quickly, someday the elm seeds will never stop falling.

. . .

Farewell clouds low or racing, farewell rain farewell birch stands, farewell legs and farewell arms, farewell hands.

. . .

I will arise and go now, running, though soon trip and fall at the feet of escape.

. . .

You think you are haunted, but what's haunting you is still alive, still alive inside of you.

. . .

The butterfly wings seemed to accuse me of staring too long, of letting my life fly by.

. . .

Health is a solid, right? Happiness a liquid? Is that it? Or is it all just vapor?

. . .

What if death is just a succubus come to suck us off in the dark of night?

. . .

In the video footage of yesterday's tsunami, several busses floated past the worried face of Jordan drowning.

See You Soon

In the gutter I found a lorgnette covered over with worms and looking knowingly up at me.

I guess someday I'll be working in the garden and the morning glory will pull *me* out.

We perfect such sly revisions, remembering to forget the faint sewage smells and babies crying just off stage.

. . .

To Determine What Went Wrong
I had hoped I could see, at least once, an instant replay before I had to leave.

. . .

I knew I would die, yet all my life I lived like an ape in a cage.

. . .

Today I realized (again) that yesterday was a dream I'll one day soon regret merely sleepwalking through.

. . .

All day I sat, staring, watching all day the rain fall, all day the others all working.

. . .

I held the water in my hands as long as I could, I watched it slip through.

. . .

Imitating the elegant movement of the spiral staircase I tripped and fell dumbly down the spiral stairs.

. . .

You think time can be saved? . . . Hmmf. Best to drink as much of it as you can.

. . .

I prefer a creek or something constantly running away, something that, by its running, stays the same.

All my life was spent asking "where to next," until now, wondering where the hell I've been.

. . .

Though I think I'm ageing rather gracefully, I would sell my soul to see those birds again.

. . .

I've probably said enough to get me into hell, but I admit I can't resist the pleasure.

. . .

At the oracle I found I had nothing really to ask, nothing really I hadn't been told.

. . .

I've spent most my life trying to find a fog thick enough wherein I could lose myself.

. . .

I've drowned so many times that all my corpses have made an island where I can relax.

. . .

One day we'll realize it's bright outside and we've been sitting on the couch our entire lives.

. . .

In retrospect, I realize that—inconceivably—I've lived most of my life in absentia: some dim elsewhere.

. . .

All I wanted was to breathe in, to be mesmerized by some silly little flower or stone.

It's funny how we worry over this or that, and then we die, and then it's fine.

I had a dream where I was a single reed in a giant marsh singing, singing, singing.

Said the Corpse
I admit the briars tangled in my hair but I didn't mind that they left me there.

Leaf
In falling I found a form of quiet calm, and then an endless still that lasted forever.

Jordan turned to stone so we drilled a hole through her and made her a garden statue.

I suppose I'll regret spending so much time staring at the plum branches waving in the wind.

I wonder what the Marx Brothers look like now and if they'll ever laugh or sing again.

I woke up covered in mud, roots fast around me, not a single word on my tongue.

One of these days the sun will just not come up, not rise at all, then what?

. . .

Some neighbor cut their grass and all of us smelled cut grass again for the first time.

. . .

Neither the depth nor the smell of my corpse kept the worms from wriggling in and eating.

. . .

Why do we assume dogs were buried with the ancient Etruscans, and not the other way around.

. . .

When the quince leafs out it won't remember flowering, and when you leave you won't remember living.

. . .

I spent most of my life thinking, writing, and philosophizing about dying, and then I did it.

. . .

Those white swan-like angels showered by golden light are a sweet sleight of hand disguising endless night.

. . .

Something like water dropping, first over one stone, then another stone, then pooling here at the end.

. . .

Someday we'll live in a place where the sun comes up every morning, every morning young again.

How A Breeze Begins
I dreamt my grandmother twitched in her grave, disturbing the roots of the maple arching over her.

Here begins the marsh, sleepless, a slavery of plants where we've found ourselves tied by the roots.

I beached the sloop on the muddy bank, stepped out, sank waist deep in muck, sludge, porridge.

Not until the bells tolled for me did I realize just how much I had been alive.

Jordan woke on the couch to find the TV on and God saying "show's over, goodnight everybody."

The bee hit the glass, then dropped down onto the window sill, still as a fishing lure.

I thought it was easy then, in the cloud light, walking around scribbling little sketches of crows.

People think that dying is somehow leaving your body. But it's not. Dying is *becoming* your body.

Final thought before I go: this was a florescent festival of Fabergé, every day a magic show.

I bent to smell the shrub's wild blooming madness, but
all of its flowers fell into darkness.

Here we go, loafing on the Spanish Steps, fields of filth
and tourists babbling obscenities all around.

I woke up and walked over, through the clouds, to the
floral couch and fell back asleep.

You have to be fearless in your confidence; when you're
dead you won't care what they've said.

Here lies another fool who struck heavy blows hoping to
make soft sibilant sounds of gentle lovely.

We walked all night, through heavy trees even, to get to
this walking, again, same as before.

When I woke the bees were thick humming dizzy work-
ing the bells of heather along the hill.

I'll be the one walking through the marsh grass, my eyes
welling up with shorebirds and clouds.

I will arise and go now, and go to, arise and go to, arise,
arise, and go.

Know thyself, we are told, know thyself, then what?
Know thyself, then watch thyself rot and disappear.

. . .

I will sit here listening to the marsh grass rush, nothing
else, just listening, listening and listing.

. . .

The yelling finally faded when I heard the gentle ringing
of pebbles softly landing on my grave.

. . .

What did you do? I walked and watched the crow, the
clouds, and corylopsis with confused adoration.

. . .

Here Lies Me
I was only guilty of drunkenness once . . . only once . . .
that time being the time I was alive.

A FUR COAT IN SUMMER

The aphorism is a delightfully stinging form: "Life is a pill which none of us can bear to swallow without gilding" (Samuel Johnson); "How pleasant life would be if it ended a little before death" (Adolfo Bioy Casares); "A man must swallow a toad every morning if he wishes to be sure of finding nothing still more disgusting before the day is over" (Sébastien-Roch Nicolas Chamfort). Aphorists from Diogenes the Dog to La Rochefoucauld to Sarah Manguso have been cynics, perhaps because, as they say, "the truth hurts" (though that's more of a proverb). What seems to unite all aphorists is the intent to produce useful, portable little nuggets of truth, no matter how unpleasant. Granted these are personal truths, but we accept them as data points for sorting through life's universally difficult questions about love, friendship, old age, death, etc.

Aphorisms are precise and definitive. Sarah Levine calls them "conclusions detached from tedious argument"; Francis Bacon found them useful as scientific propositions, and felt that "There is nothing more exact"; Friedrich von Schlegel praised the aphorism as the "True form of Universal Philosophy." In a word, the aphorism, like the scientific hypothesis, is supposed to be of use to us.

In *All the Useless Things are Mine*, Thomas Walton performs feats of brevity, wit, and cynicism, like all of history's best aphorists (there's even a chapter called "Bitter Pills"). At the same time Walton also subverts the form. The result has plenty of aphoristic music, but the "advice" offered us directly or implicitly is perverse, incongruous, counterintuitive, perhaps even hazardous to our health. Walton slips quickly away from the aphorism into other modes altogether, pushing beyond irony into deadpan humor and beyond wistfulness into pure birdsong. Here we find one-liners ("Our babysitter drinks whiskey and is usually late, but we don't mind, we don't have a baby"); seventeen-word, haiku-like poems evoking the stark, image-driven aesthetic of William Carlos Williams ("The frost seized last night the scarlet petals of the geranium spilling through the iron balcony"); and tableaux in miniature ("I spent the morning leaping from cloud to cloud, finding good in every god I came across").

As Walton waltzes between these diverse modes, he adheres strictly to the "seventeen" form, which lends each entry more or less equal weight: the bawdy joke about cat feces gets as much air-time as the love poem written to a hydrangea bush. "To some extent, each sentence has to be the whole story," wrote Lyn Hejinian in *My Life*, and this seems to be Walton's project, too. What can the human mind do with seventeen words? How many different shapes can it make, tones can it hit, songs can it sing? Walton's is a search each time for poetic truth, for musical truth. If it sounds true, we feel he is satisfied—especially when the statement is absurd: "I interviewed in a soft sheer fabric made from fibrous pineapple leaves but didn't get the job!"

Walton seems to have cast off the trappings of wisdom in favor of whimsy—to prefer fantasy, absurdity, pornography, buffoonery, and ecstatic song to staking any claim on truth. The poet admits that he and his writings are perhaps useless ("Here again on the couch, scribbling little nothings at the clouds, the city going on without me") and yet he doesn't seem to care at all. His sensibility reminds me of that of the quirky ancient Chinese sage known as Zhuangzi who used paradox, puns, jokes, metaphors, and incongruence to "shuck off all du-

alistic modes of thinking" and to free us from "petty knowl-
edge," as in this vignette:

> Master Tung-kuo asked Chuang Tzu, "This thing called
> the Way—where does it exist?"
>
> Chuang Tzu said, "There's no place it does not exist."
>
> "Come," said Master Tung-kuo, "you must be more spe-
> cific!"
>
> "It is in the ant."
>
> "As low as that?"
>
> "It is in the panic grass."
>
> "But that's lower still."
>
> "It is in the tiles and shards."
>
> "How can it be so low?"
>
> "It is in the piss and shit!"
>
> Master Tung-kuo made no reply.
>
> (Watson, 1968, *The Complete Works of Chuang Tzu*, pp. 240–1)

The implication here, of course, is that Master Tung-kuo has
become enlightened! He has arrived at a glorious sense of one-
ness that his discriminating mind had kept at bay.

Zhuangzi argues that the useful and the useless are also
one. Upon catching a snake, one culture thinks the snake valu-
able and another thinks it useless. A fan in the winter is use-
less, as is a fur coat in the summer. Fruit trees are thought to
be useful and valuable, explains Zhuangzi, writing in the voice
of an oak tree, but "as soon as their fruit is ripe, they are torn
apart and subjected to abuse . . . Their utility makes life mis-
erable for them," and for this reason the oak tree has all its life
"sought to be useless."

The seventeen drawings that appear in these pages also seek the liberation of being useless. Douglas Miller's portraits of common household objects and lowly animals—low as the ant, low as the panic grass and shards—have been left unfinished, which on first glance undermines their authority. Miller focuses, for example, on one piercing eye of a black cat, or the partial head of an owl, and leaves the rest of the body untouched. A paintbrush hovers fearlessly in the middle of the empty white page, lacking painter, canvas, context, or conclusion. In their "sketchiness," Miller's subjects come alive—to a heightened degree—as if they were still emerging, still humbly in creation.

Zhuangzi makes a proposition (in one word short of seventeen, unfortunately) that sings happily at the heart of this book: "Everyone knows the advantage of being useful, yet no one knows the advantage of being useless!"

—*Elizabeth Cooperman*

Douglas Miller is a professional artist whose drawings have been exhibited in galleries and museums throughout the United States. Additionally, Douglas does freelance illustrations as well as private and corporate commissions. Recently, Douglas received the prestigious Al Smith Fellowship for Visual Arts from the Kentucky Arts Council and the National Endowment for the Arts and a national award from *American Artist: Drawing* magazine. His artwork is in the collection of the Evansville Museum of Arts and Science, the University of Louisville, the Speed School of Engineering, and numerous private collections throughout the world. Douglas lives and works in Louisville, Kentucky.

Thomas Walton is author of the anti-lyric-essay lyric essay *The World Is All That Does Befall Us* (Ravenna Press, 2019), the micro-chapbook *A Name Is Just A Mane* (Rinky Dink, 2016), and, with Elizabeth Cooperman, the tesselated essay/poem *The Last Mosaic* (Sagging Meniscus Press, 2018). His work has appeared in *ZYZZYVA*, *Delmar*, *Timberline Review*, *Rivet*, *The Chaos Journal*, *Queen Mob's Teahouse*, *Bombay Gin*, *Pontoon*, and other magazines. He is one of three editors of the bilingual poetry anthology *Make It True Meets Medusario* (Pleasure Boat Studio, 2019). He lives in Seattle, where he builds gardens and edits *PageBoy Magazine*.